THIS CANDLEWICK BOOK BELONGS TO:

Copyright © 1993 by John Burningham

First U.S. paperback edition in this form 2000

The Library of Congress has cataloged the hardcover edition as follows:

Burningham, John.
Harvey Slumfenburger's Christmas present / John Burningham.
— 1st U.S. ed.

Summary: On discovering late Christmas Eve that he has forgotten
to deliver one present, Santa Claus wearily makes his way in a variety of conveyances
to the top of the Roly Poly Mountain to deliver it.

ISBN 1-56402-246-3 (hardcover)

1. Santa Claus—Juvenile fiction. [1. Santa Claus—Fiction.
2. Christmas—Fiction. 3. Vehicles—Fiction.] I. Title.

PZ7.B936Har   1993   92–54957

[E]—dc20

ISBN 0-7636-1378-9 (paperback)

2 4 6 8 10 9 7 5 3 1

Printed in Hong Kong

This book was typeset in Galliard.
The illustrations were done in pen and watercolor.

Candlewick Press
2067 Massachusetts Avenue
Cambridge, Massachusetts 02140

Harvey Slumfenburger's
Christmas
Present

John Burningham

CANDLEWICK PRESS
CAMBRIDGE, MASSACHUSETTS

It was Christmas Eve.
Santa Claus and the
reindeer were home at last.
They were very tired because
they had been delivering presents
to all the children everywhere.

They had something to eat, and then Santa Claus put the reindeer to bed. One of the reindeer said it did not feel very well—maybe it had nibbled something on the way that it should not have.

Santa Claus thought that
all it needed was a good
night's sleep.

Finally Santa Claus was able to go to bed. He put on his pajamas and was just climbing into bed when he saw something that made him gasp. At the end of his bed lay his sack. Santa Claus could see the shape of one present still inside it.

Santa Claus pulled the present out of the sack. The present was Harvey Slumfenburger's.

Santa Claus knew all about Harvey Slumfenburger. He knew that Harvey Slumfenburger's parents were too poor to buy him presents. He knew that Harvey Slumfenburger only ever got one present, and that was the present that Santa Claus brought him. He knew that Harvey Slumfenburger lived in a hut at the top of the Roly Poly Mountain, which was far, far away.

Santa Claus was very tired.
The reindeer were asleep, and one of them
was not very well. But Santa Claus knew he
had to get the present to Harvey Slumfenburger.

Santa Claus put on his coat over his pajamas. He put on his boots and hat, picked up the sack with Harvey Slumfenburger's present in it, and started to walk

through the cold winter night to the hut where
Harvey Slumfenburger lived at the top of the
Roly Poly Mountain, which was far, far away.

Santa Claus had not gone very far when he met a man with an airplane. "Excuse me," he said, "my name is Santa Claus. I still have one present left in my sack, which is for Harvey Slumfenburger, the little boy who lives in a hut at the top of the Roly Poly Mountain, which is far, far away. And it will soon be Christmas Day."

"Get in my plane," said the man, "and I will take you as far as I can." The airplane took off and flew through the night sky toward the Roly Poly Mountain.

Heavy snow began to fall.

"I am so sorry, Santa Claus," said the man. "I cannot fly my airplane any farther in this snow." The plane bumped and skidded across the ground and finally came to a halt. "But if you go to the garage that lies over the hill, there is a man with a jeep. Maybe he can help you."

Santa Claus set off through the snow. He went over the hill to the garage where there was the man with the jeep. "Excuse me," he said, "my name is Santa Claus. I still have one present left in my sack, which is for Harvey Slumfenburger, the little boy who lives in a hut at the top of the Roly Poly Mountain, which is far, far away. And it will soon be Christmas Day."

"Climb in my jeep," said the man, "and I will take you as far as I can."

The jeep bounced and spun across the fields and down the road toward the Roly Poly Mountain.

But then the jeep skidded and crashed through the fence and into a tree. Santa Claus was sent tumbling into the snow.

"I am so sorry, Santa Claus," said the man. "I can take you no farther. But if you go down the hill and across the river, there is a boy with a motorbike. Maybe he can help you."

Santa Claus went down the hill and across the river and met the boy with the motorbike. "Excuse me," he said, "my name is Santa Claus. I still have one present left in my sack, which is for Harvey Slumfenburger, the little boy who lives in a hut at the top of the Roly Poly Mountain, which is far, far away. And it will soon be Christmas Day."

"We'll go on my motorbike," said the boy. "I will take you as far as I can."

The motorbike roared off along the road toward the Roly Poly Mountain.

But they had not gone very far before the
motorbike slid on some ice and they both fell off.
"I am so sorry, Santa Claus," said the boy. "The
front of my bike is all twisted, and I can take you
no farther. But if you go across the valley and
into the woods, there is a girl who has skis.
Maybe she can help you."

Santa Claus went across the valley and into the woods, where he found the girl with skis. "Excuse me," he said, "my name is Santa Claus. I still have one present left in my sack, which is for Harvey Slumfenburger, the little boy who lives in a hut at the top of the Roly Poly Mountain, which is far, far away. And it will soon be Christmas Day."

"Stand on the back of my skis," said the girl, "and I will take you as far as I can toward the Roly Poly Mountain."

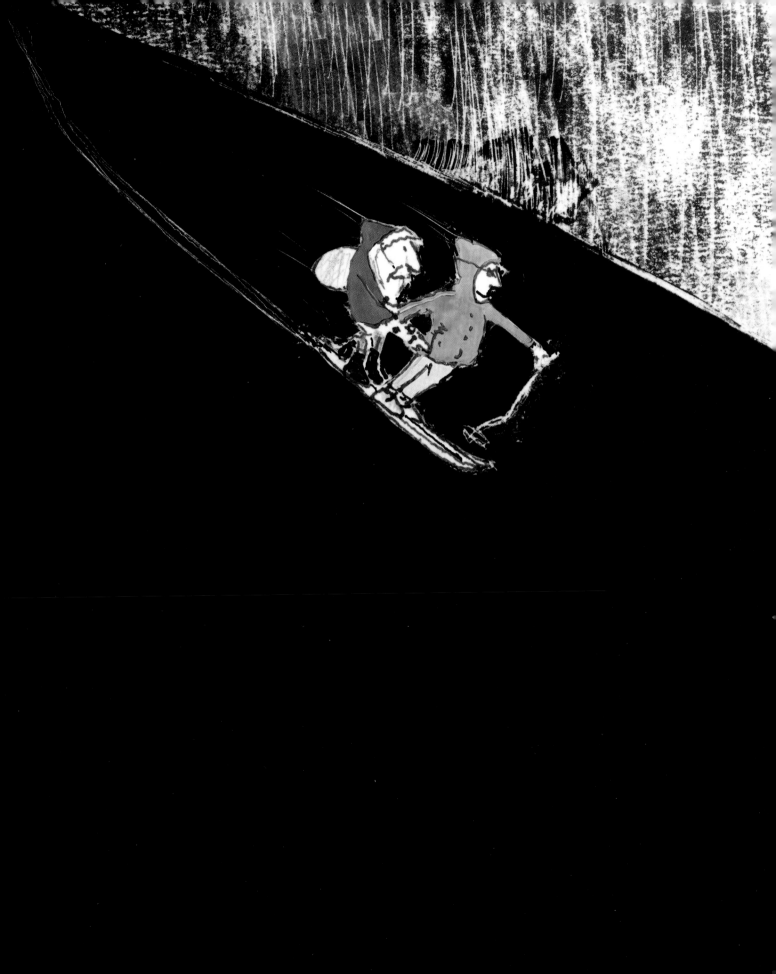

They had not gone very far when the skis broke
with a crack and they both tumbled into the snow.

"I am so sorry, Santa Claus," said the girl. "My skis are broken and I can take you no farther. But if you go up the slope and down onto the plain, you will be near the bottom of the Roly Poly Mountain, where there is a climber with a rope. Maybe he can help you."

Santa Claus went up the slope and down onto the plain, where he found the climber with the rope. "Excuse me," he said, "my name is Santa Claus. I still have one present left in my sack, which is for Harvey Slumfenburger, the little boy who lives in a hut at the top of the Roly Poly Mountain, which is far, far away. And it will soon be Christmas Day."

"Hold on to my rope," said the climber, "and I will take you as far as I can up the Roly Poly Mountain."

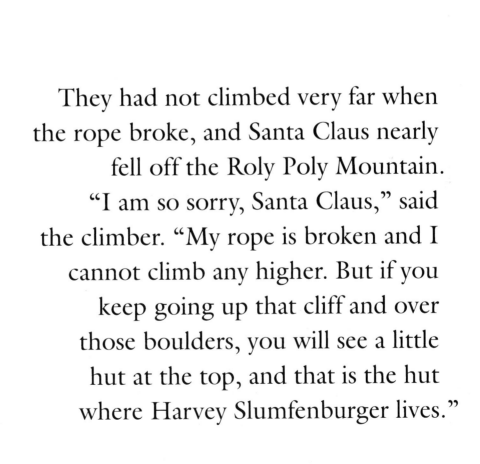

They had not climbed very far when
the rope broke, and Santa Claus nearly
fell off the Roly Poly Mountain.
"I am so sorry, Santa Claus," said
the climber. "My rope is broken and I
cannot climb any higher. But if you
keep going up that cliff and over
those boulders, you will see a little
hut at the top, and that is the hut
where Harvey Slumfenburger lives."

Santa Claus kept going up the cliff and over the boulders and finally arrived at the hut where Harvey Slumfenburger lived.

Santa Claus
climbed onto the
roof and down
the chimney . . . .

and put the present in Harvey Slumfenburger's stocking.

Then Santa Claus set
off on the long
journey home.

Santa Claus checked
that the reindeer
were all right and
tucked in bed.

And as the sun began to rise on Christmas
morning, Santa Claus climbed into bed and
was soon fast asleep.

In the hut at the top of the Roly Poly Mountain, which is far, far away, a little boy, whose name was Harvey Slumfenburger, reached for the stocking on the end of his bed and took out his present.

I wonder what it was.